D1281481

Dido, Queen of Carthage

Christopher Marlowe, Thomas Nash

BIBLIOLIFE

DIDO, QUEEN OF CARTHAGE.

A TRAGEDY,

BY

CHRISTOPHER MARLOWE, AND THOMAS NASH.

LONDON:

PRINTED FOR HURST, ROBINSON, AND CO.,

90, CHEAPSIDE, AND 8, PALL MALL;

AND ARCHIBALD CONSTABLE AND CO., EDINBURGH.

MDCCCXXV.

LONDON:
Printed by D. S Maurice, Fenchurch Street.

PERSONS REPRESENTED.

JUPITER.
GANYMEDE.
CUPID.
MERCURY.
ÆNEAS.
ASCANIUS.
ACHATES.
ILIONEUS.
CLOANTHUS.
SERGESTUS.
IARBAS.

JUNO.
VENUS.
DIDO.
ANNA.
NURSE.

Lords, &c.

THOMAS NASH.

Thomas Nash was born at the small sea-port town of Leostoff, in Suffolk, probably about the year 1564. He was, as he himself informs us, descended from a family who were seated in Hertfordshire. He became a student of St. John's College, Cambridge, and took his Batchelor's degree in 1585. We have assigned his birth to the year 1564, partly on the authority of a pamphlet, published in 1597, entitled *The trimming of Thomas Nash, Gentleman, by the high tituled Patron Don Richardo de Medico Campo, Barber Chirurgeon to Trinity College, in Cambridge*. This production states that he left College at seven years' standing, and before he had taken his Master's degree, about the year 1587; a statement, on the accuracy of which we may probably rely, with respect to such a fact as this, although proceeding from the pen of an adversary. Assuming, therefore, that Nash went to College at the age of sixteen, (about the usual time,) his birth would, according to this authority, have been in the year above mentioned. From Cambridge, he proceeded to London. In the literary

warfare between the Puritans, under the name of Martin
Mar-prelate, and the Church, Nash ranked himself on the
side of the establishment, and took an active part in the
controversy   He attacked them in their own style, and
by the skilful application of his peculiar talents of ridicule
and invective, he was chiefly instrumental in silencing them.
Amongst his productions in this contest, were *Pap with
a hatchet, or a fig for my godson, or crack me this nut.   To
be sold at the Crab-tree Cudgel, in Thwack-Coat Lane.*
and *An almond for a Parrot, or an alms for Martin.* The
following are also supposed to have been written by
him: *A counter-scuffle given to Martin Junior —Martin's
month's mind.—The return of the renowned Pasquill of
England.*

The pamphlet before quoted asserts that Nash, whilst
at College, had assisted in writing a show called *Terminus
et non Terminus,* for which, the person who had been con-
cerned with him was expelled ; and that Nash himself was,
at that time, (1597,) in prison for having written a play called *The Isle of Dogs* ; neither of which facts, consider-
ing the freedom and severity of his satire, are improbable.

Nash was one of the choice wits and boon companions of
his day : if he originally possessed any patrimony, it was
soon consumed in the dissipations of a town life, and he
was reduced to dependance on literary patronage and the
produce of his pen. That the latter was fertile enough,
must be allowed, but its fruits were not sufficient to supply
his wants. He commences his *Pierce Pennilesse, his sup-
plication to the Devil,* with a very touching description

of his situation. "Having," says he, "spent many years
in studying how to live, and lived a long time without mo-
ney; having tired my youth with folly, and surfeited my
mind with vanity, I began at length to look back to repent-
ance, and addressed my endeavours to prosperity; but all
in vain, I sat up late and rose early, contended with the
cold and conversed with scarcity; for all my labours turned
to loss, my vulgar Muse was despised and neglected, my
pains not regarded, or slightly rewarded, and I myself, in
prime of my best wit, laid open to poverty."

From the following passage, it is not improbable that he
had experienced the bounty of Sir Philip Sidney: "Gentle
Sir Philip Sidney, thou knewest what pains, what toils,
what travail conduct to perfection: well couldest thou give
every virtue his encouragement, every art his due, every
writer his desert, 'cause none more virtuous, witty, or lear-
ned, than thyself. But thou art dead in thy grave, and hast
left too few successors of thy glory, too few to cherish the
sons of the Muses, or water those budding hopes with their
plenty, which thy bounty erst planted."

Nash appears to have been very much in need of a patron
at this time: in the production just quoted, he holds out
flattering promises of what he would do, if any Mecænas
would extend his bounty to him: "Gentles," says he, "it
is not your lay Chronigraphers, that write of nothing but
Mayors and Sheriffs, and the Dear Year, and the Great
Frost, that can endow your names with never dated glory: for
they want the wings of choice words to fly to heaven, which
we have: they cannot sweeten a discourse, or wrest admira-

tion from men reading, as we can, reporting the meanest
accident.   Poetry is the honey of all flowers, the quint-
essence of all sciences, the marrow of all wits, and the very
phrase of angels : how much better is it, then, to have an
elegant lawyer to plead one's cause, than a strutting towns-
man that looseth himself in his tale, and doth nothing but
make legs ; so much it is better for a nobleman or gentleman, to have his honour's story related, and his deeds em-
blazon'd by a Poet than a Citizen,   *   *   *   *   *   *   *
*   *   *   *   *   *   *   *   *   *   *   *   *   *   *

   "For my part, I do challenge no praise of learning to myself; yet have I worn a gown in the university : but this I dare
presume, that, if any Mecænas bind me to him by his bounty,
or extend some sound liberality to me worth the speaking of,
I will do him as much honour as any Poet of my beardless
years shall in England.   Not that I am so confident what
I can do, but that I attribute so much to my thankful
mind above others, which, I am persuaded, would enable
me to work miracles.   On the contrary side, if I be evil
intreated, or sent away with a flea in mine ear, let him
look that I will rail on him soundly: not for an hour or a
day, while the injury is fresh in my memory, but in some
elaborate polished poem, which I will leave to the world
when I am dead, to be a living image to all ages, of his
beggarly parsimony and ignoble illiberality : and let him
not (whatsoever he be) measure the weight of my words
by this book, where I write *Quicquid in buccam veniret*, as
fast as my hand can trot; but I have terms (if I be vext)
laid in steep in aquafortis, and gunpowder, that shall

rattle through the skies, and make an earthquake in a peasant ears.   Put case (since I am not yet out of the theme
of wrath) that some tired jade belonging to the press,
whom I never wronged in my life, hath named me ex-
pressly in print (as I will not do him), and accused me of
want of learning, upbraiding me for reviving in an epistle
of mine the reverend memory of Sir Thomas Moore, Sir
John Cheeke, Doctor Watson, Doctor Haddon, Doctor
Carr, Master Ascham, as if they were no meat but for
his mastership's mouth, but some such as the son of a
ropemaker were worthy to mention them.   To shew how
I can rail, thus I would begin to rail on him.—Thou that
hadst thy hood turned over thy ears when thou wert a
Batchelor, for abusing of Aristotle, and setting him upon
the school gates, painted with asses' ears on his head, is it
any discredit for me, thou great baboon, thou pigmy
braggart, thou pamphleter of nothing but Peans, to be
censured by thee, that has scorned the prince of philoso-
phers; thou, that in thy dialogues sold'st honey for a half-
penny, and the choicest writers extant for cues a piece;
that cam'st to the logic schools when thou wert a fresh-
man, and writ'st phrases · off with thy gown and untruss!
for I mean to lash thee mightily."

And so he goes on in a strain of vituperation and invective, of which few writers can furnish an example.   This
was the commencement of those bitter conflicts between
Nash and Gabriel Harvey, with which the town was amus-
ed, and which, at length, attained such a pitch of violence
and animosity, that the Archbishop of Canterbury issued

an order, "that all Nash's books, and Harvey's books, be taken wheresoever they may be found, and that none of the said books be ever printed hereafter." These books have, in consequence, become exceeding rare. In this literary combat, Nash, with his fluent wit, his light and airy evolutions, and his caustic invective, had decidedly the advantage over the unwieldy pedantry, the clumsy but bitter abuse, and cynical hatred, of Harvey; and almost literally performed his boast, that if you "look on his head you shall find a grey hair for every line I have writ against him;" and he adds, "and you shall have all his beard white too by the time he hath read over this book."* Before his death, however, Nash, if we are to believe his Dedication of *Christ's Tears over Jerusalem*, addressed to Lady Elizabeth Carey, grew weary of this employment. "A hundred unfortunate farewells," says he, "to fantastical satyrism, in whose veins heretofore I mispent my spirit, and prodigally conspired against good hours. Nothing is there now so much in my vows as to be at peace with all men, and make submissive amends where I have most displeased."

This piquant satirist died, it is supposed, in 1600 or 1601, he having published a pamphlet in 1599, and being spoken of as dead in *The Return from Parnassus*, which is supposed to have been written in 1602, and was acted in 1606.

Nash enjoyed a great reputation amongst the wits of his time. Dr. Lodge calls him "the true English Aretine."

---

* Have with you to Saffron-Walden, or Gabriel Harvey's Hunt is up, 1594.

Drayton says of him—

> " And surely, Nash, tho' he a proser were,
> A branch of laurel yet deserves to bear ;
> Sharply satirick was he, and that way
> He went, since that his being, to this day,
> Few have attempted ; and I surely think
> Those words shall hardly be set down in ink,
> Shall scorch and blast, so as his could, when he
> Would inflict vengeance."

And in the play of *The Return from Parnassus*, he is characterized as "a fellow that carried the deadly stock* in his pen, whose Muse was armed with a gag-tooth, and his pen possessed with Hercules' furies," which is succeeded by the following lines :—

> " Let all his faults sleep with his mournful chest,
> And then for ever with his ashes rest ;
> His style was witty, though he had some gall ;
> Something he might have mended ; so may all .
> Yet this I say, that, for a mother wit,
> Few men have ever seen the like of it."

His dramatic productions consist of *Summer's last Will and Testament*, a Comedy, 4to., 1600 ; *The Isle of Dogs*, never printed ; and *Dido, Queen of Carthage*, a Tragedy, 4to., 1594, in which he was assisted by Marlowe.

Nash does not appear, from the specimens he has left us, to have possessed much dramatic talent · his *Summer's last Will and Testament* is more closely allied to satire than the drama ; partakes more of invective than of passion ; and *Dido*, of which he, probably, wrote the greater part,

* Stocco, a long rapier

is little more than a narrative taken from Virgil, con-
structed according to the form of a drama, but containing
little of the essence of that species of composition.

THE TRAGEDIE OF DIDO,

QUEEN OF CARTHAGE;

PLAYED BY THE CHILDREN OF HER MAIESTIE'S CHAPPELL.

WRITTEN BY

CHRISTOPHER MARLOWE, AND THOMAS NASH, GENT

Actors.

JUPITER.	ASCANIUS.
GANIMEDE.	DIDO.
VENUS.	ANNA.
CUPID.	ACHATES.
JUNO.	ILIONEUS.
MERCURIE, OR	IARBAS.
HERMES.	CLOANTHES.
ÆNEAS.	SERGESTUS.

AT LONDON:

PRINTED, BY THE WIDDOWE ORWIN, FOR THOMAS WOODCOCKE,

AND ARE TO BE SOLDE AT HIS SHOP, IN PAULE'S CHURCH-YARD,

AT THE SIGNE OF THE BLACKE BEARE.

1594.

DIDO, QUEEN OF CARTHAGE,

Is included in this collection for two reasons: first, the early period at which it was written, (before 1592); and, secondly, the extreme rarity of it; there being, we believe, only two copies known to exist in England. Possessing very little intrinsic merit as a play, it is now reprinted chiefly for the purpose of illustrating the progress of dramatic art in this country, which forms part of the design of the present work.

DIDO, QUEEN OF CARTHAGE.

————

ACT I. SCENE I.

Here the curtains draw :—there is discovered JUPITER *dandling*
   GANYMEDE *upon his knee, and* MERCURY *lying asleep*

   Jup. COME, gentle Ganymede, and play with me;
I love thee well, say Juno what she will.

   Gan. I am much better for your worthless love,
That will not shield me from her shrewish blows:
To-day, when as I fill'd into your cups,
And held the cloth of pleasance while you drank,
She reach'd me such a rap for that I spill'd,
As made the blood run down about mine ears.

   Jup. What! dares she strike the darling of my
         thoughts?
By Saturn's soul, and this earth threat'ning air,
That, shaken thrice, makes nature's buildings quake,
I vow, if she but once frown on thee more,
To hang her, meteor-like, 'twixt heaven and earth,
And bind her hand and foot with golden cords,

B

As once I did for harming Hercules !

    Gan. Might I but see that pretty sport a-foot,
O how would I with Helen's brother laugh,
And bring the Gods to wonder at the game.
Sweet Jupiter ! if e'er I pleas'd thine eye,
Or seemed fair wall'd-in with eagle's wings,
Grace my immortal beauty with this boon,
And I will spend my time in thy bright arms

    Jup. What is't, sweet wag, I should deny thy youth ?
Whose face reflects such pleasure to mine eyes,
As I, exhal'd with thy fire-darting beams,
Have oft driven back the horses of the night,
When as they would have hal'd thee from my sight.
Sit on my knee, and call for thy content,
Controul proud fate, and cut the thread of time :
Why, are not all the gods at thy command,
And heaven and earth the bounds of thy delight ?
Vulcan shall dance to make thee laughing sport,
And my nine daughters sing when thou art sad ;
From Juno's bird I'll pluck her spotted pride,
To make thee fans wherewith to cool thy face ;
And Venus' swans shall shed their silver down,
To sweeten out the slumbers of thy bed
Hermes no more shall shew the world his wings,
If that thy fancy in his feathers dwell,
But as this one I'll tear them all from him,
Do thou but say, " their colour pleaseth me."
Hold here, my little love, these linked gems,
My Juno wore upon her marriage day,
Put thou about thy neck, my own sweet heart,

And trick thy arms and shoulders with my theft.

   Gan. I would have a jewel for mine ear,
And a fine broach to put into my hat,
And then I'll hug with you a hundred times.

    Jup. And shalt have, Ganymede, if thou wilt be my
      love.

Enter VENUS.

   Ven. Aye, this is it; you can sit toying there,
And playing with that female wanton boy,
While my Æneas wanders on the seas,
And rests a prey to every billow's pride.
Juno, false Juno, in her chariot's pomp,
Drawn through the heavens by steeds of Boreas' brood,
Made Hebe to direct her airy wheels
Into the windy country of the clouds;
Where, finding Æolus intrench'd with storms,
And guarded with a thousand grisly ghosts,
She humbly did beseech him for our bane,
And charg'd him drown my son with all his train.
Then 'gan the winds break ope their brazen doors,
And all Æolia to be up in arms;
Poor Troy must now be sack'd upon the sea,
And Neptune's waves be envious men of war;
Epeus' horse to Ætna's hill transform'd,
Prepared stands to wreck their wooden walls;
And Æolus, like Agamemnon, sounds
The surges, his fierce soldiers, to the spoil:
See how the night, Ulysses-like, comes forth,
And intercepts the day as Dolon erst!

Ah, me! the stars surpris'd, like Rhesus' steeds,
Are drawn by darkness forth Astræa's tents.
What shall I do to save thee, my sweet boy?
When as the waves do threat our crystal world,
And Proteus, raising hills of floods on high,
Intends, ere long, to sport him in the sky.
False Jupiter! reward'st thou virtue so?
What! is not piety exempt from woe?
Then die, Æneas, in thy innocence,
Since that religion hath no recompence.

   Jup. Content thee, Cytherea, in thy care,
Since thy Æneas' wand'ring fate is firm,
Whose weary limbs shall shortly make repose
In those fair walls I promis'd him of yore :
But first in blood must his good fortune bud,
Before he be the lord of Turnus' town,
Or force her smile, that hitherto hath frown'd :
Three winters shall he with the Rutiles war,
And, in the end, subdue them with his sword ,
And full three summers likewise shall he waste,
In managing those fierce barbarian minds ;
Which once perform'd, poor Troy, so long suppress'd,
From forth her ashes shall advance her head,
And flourish once again, that erst was dead .
But bright Ascanius' beauties better work,
Who with the sun divides one radiant shape,
Shall build his throne amidst those starry towers,
That earth-born Atlas, groaning, underprops :
No bounds, but heaven, shall bound his empery,
Whose azur'd gates, enchased with his name,

Shall make the morning haste her grey uprise,
To feed her eyes with his engraven fame.
Thus, in stout Hector's race, three hundred years
The Roman sceptre royal shall remain,
Till that a princess, priest-conceiv'd by Mars,
Shall yield to dignity a double birth,
Who will eternise Troy in their attempts.

    Ven. How may I credit these thy flattering terms,
When yet both sea and sand beset their ships,
And Phœbus, as in Stygian pools, refrains
To taint his tresses in the Tyrrhene main?

    Jup. I will take order for that presently :—
Hermes, awake! and haste to Neptune's realm;
Whereas the wind-god, warring now with fate,
Besiege the offspring of our kingly loins,
Charge him from me to turn his stormy powers,
And fetter them in Vulcan's sturdy brass,
That durst thus proudly wrong our kinsman's peace.
Venus, farewell! thy son shall be our care;
Come, Ganymede, we must about this gear.

                    [exeunt Jupiter and Ganymede.

    Ven. Disquiet seas, lay down your swelling looks,
And court Æneas with your calmy cheer,
Whose beauteous burden well might make you proud,
Had not the heavens, conceiv'd with hell-born clouds,
Veil'd his resplendent glory from your view;
For my sake, pity him, Oceanus,
That erst-while issued from thy wat'ry loins,
And had my being from thy bubbling froth.
Triton, I know, hath fill'd his trump with Troy,

And, therefore, will take pity on his toil,
And call both Thetis and Cymodoce,
To succour him in this extremity.

Enter ÆNEAS, ASCANIUS, ACHATES, and one or two more.

What ! do I see my son now come on shore ?
Venus, how art thou compass'd with content,
The while thine eyes attract their sought-for joys :
Great Jupiter ! still honour'd may'st thou be,
For this so friendly aid in time of need!
Here in this bush disguised will I stand,
Whiles my Æneas spends himself in plaints,
And heaven and earth with his unrest acquaints.

Æn. You sons of care, companions of my course,
Priam's misfortune follows us by sea,
And Helen's rape doth haunt us at the heels.
How many dangers have we overpast ?
Both barking Scylla, and the sounding rocks,
The Cyclops' shelves, and grim Ceraunia's seat,
Have you o'ergone, and yet remain alive.
Pluck up your hearts, since fate still rests our friend,
And changing heavens may those good days return,
Which Pergama did vaunt in all her pride.

Acha. Brave Prince of Troy, thou only art our god,
That, by thy virtues, free'st us from-annoy,
And mak'st our hopes survive to cunning joys !
Do thou but smile, and cloudy heaven will clear,
Whose night and day descendeth from thy brows :
Though we be now in extreme misery,
And rest the map of weather-beaten woe,

Yet shall the aged sun shed forth his air,
To make us live unto our former heat,
And every beast the forest doth send forth,
Bequeath her young ones to our scanted food.

Asca. Father, I faint; good father, give me meat.

Æn. Alas! sweet boy, thou must be still awhile,
Till we have fire to dress the meat we kill'd;
Gentle Achates, reach the tinder-box,
That we may make a fire to warm us with,
And roast our new found victuals on this shore.

Ven. See what strange arts necessity finds out;
How near, my sweet Æneas, art thou driven.

Æn. Hold; take this candle, and go light a fire;
You shall have leaves and windfall boughs enow
Near to these woods, to roast your meat withal:
Ascanius, go and dry thy drenched limbs,
While I with my Achates roam abroad,
To know what coast the wind hath driv'n us on,
Or whether men or beasts inhabit it.

Acha. The air is pleasant, and the soil most fit
For cities, and society's supports;
Yet much I marvel that I cannot find
No steps of men imprinted in the earth.

Ven. Now is the time for me to play my part: [*aside.*
Ho, young men! saw you, as you came,
Any of all my sisters wand'ring here,
Having a quiver girded to her side,
And clothed in a spotted leopard's skin?

Æn. I neither saw nor heard of any such;
But what may I, fair virgin, call your name?

Whose looks set forth no mortal form to view,
Nor speech bewrays ought human in thy birth;
Thou art a goddess that delud'st our eyes,
And shroud'st thy beauty in this borrow'd shape;
But whether thou the sun's bright sister be,
Or one of chaste Diana's fellow nymphs,
Live happy in the height of all content,
And lighten our extremes with this one boon,
As to instruct us under what good heaven
We breathe as now, and what this world is call'd
On which, by tempests' fury, we are cast?
Tell us, O tell us, that are ignorant;
And this right hand shall make thy altars crack
With mountain heaps of milk-white sacrifice.

   Ven. Such honour, stranger, do I not affect;
It is the use for Tyrian maids to wear
Their bow and quiver in this modest sort,
And suit themselves in purple for the nonce,
That they may trip more lightly o'er the lawns,
And overtake the tusked boar in chase.
But for the land whereof thou dost enquire,
It is the Punick kingdom, rich and strong,
Adjoining on Agenor's stately town,
The kingly seat of Southern Lybia,
Whereas Sidonian Dido rules as queen.
But what are you that ask of me these things?
Whence may you come, or whither will you go?

   Æn. Of Troy am I, Æneas is my name;
Who, driv'n by war from forth my native world,
Put sails to sea to seek out Italy;

And my divine descent from sceptr'd Jove:
With twice twelve Phrygian ships I plough'd the deep,
And made that way my mother Venus led;
But of them all scarce seven do anchor safe,
And they so wrack'd and welter'd by the waves,
As every tide tilts 'twixt their oaken sides;
And all of them, unburthen'd of their load,
Are ballasted with billows' wat'ry weight.
But hapless I, God wot! poor and unknown,
Do trace these Lybian deserts all despis'd,
Exil'd forth Europe and wide Asia both,
And have not any coverture but heaven.

Ven. Fortune hath favour'd thee, whate'er thou be,
In sending thee unto this courteous coast:
In God's name, on! and haste thee to the court,
Where Dido will receive ye with her smiles;
And for thy ships, which thou supposest lost,
Not one of them hath perish'd in the storm,
But are arrived safe, not far from hence;
And so I leave thee to thy fortune's lot,
Wishing good luck unto thy wand'ring steps.   [*exit.*

Æn. Achates, 'tis my mother that is fled;
I know her by the movings of her feet:
Stay, gentle Venus, fly not from thy son;
Too cruel! why wilt thou forsake me thus?
Or in these shades deceiv'st mine eyes so oft?
Why talk we not together hand in hand,
And tell our griefs in more familiar terms?
But thou art gone, and leav'st me here alone,
To dull the air with my discoursive moan.   [*exeunt.*

SCENE II.

Enter IARBAS, *followed by* ILIONEUS, CLOANTHUS, *and* SERGES-
TUS.

Ilio. Follow, ye Trojans! follow this brave lord,
And 'plain to him the sum of your distress.

Iar. Why, what are you, or wherefore do you sue?

Ilio. Wretches of Troy, envied of the winds,
That crave such favour at your honour's feet,
As poor distressed misery may plead :
Save, save, O save our ships from cruel fire,
That do complain the wounds of thousand waves,
And spare our lives, whom every spite pursues.
We come not, we, to wrong your Lybian gods,
Or steal your household lares from their shrines :
Our hands are not prepar'd to lawless spoil,
Nor armed to offend in any kind ;
Such force is far from our unweapon'd thoughts,
Whose fading weal, of victory forsook,
Forbids all hope to harbour near our hearts.

Iar. But tell me, Trojans, Trojans if you be,
Unto what fruitful quarters were ye bound,
Before that Boreas buckled with your sails?

Cloan. There is a place, Hesperia term'd by us,
An ancient empire, famoused for arms,
And fertile in fair Ceres' furrow'd wealth,
Which now we call Italia, of his name
That in such peace long time did rule the same.
Thither made we ;

When, suddenly, gloomy Orion rose,
And led our ships into the shallow sands ;
Whereas the southern wind, with brackish breath,
Dispers'd them all amongst the wreckful rocks ;
From thence a few of us escap'd to land ;
The rest, we fear, are folded in the floods.

Iar. Brave men at arms, abandon fruitless fears,
Since Carthage knows to entertain distress.

Serg. Aye, but the barb'rous sort do threat our ships,
And will not let us lodge upon the sands ;
In multitudes they swarm unto the shore,
And from the first earth interdict our feet.

Iar. Myself will see they shall not trouble ye :
Your men and you shall banquet in our court,
And ev'ry Trojan be as welcome here,
As Jupiter to silly Baucis' house.
Come in with me, I'll bring you to my queen,
Who shall confirm my words with further deeds.

Serg. Thanks, gentle lord, for such unlook'd-for grace ;
Might we but once more see Æneas' face,
Then would we hope to 'quite such friendly turns,
As shall surpass the wonder of our speech.   [*exeunt.*

ACT II.   SCENE I.

Enter Æneas, Achates, *and* Ascanius

Æn. Where am I now ? these should be Carthage walls.

Acha Why stands my sweet Æneas thus amaz'd?

Æn. O, my Achates! Theban Niobe,
Who, for her sons' death, wept out life and breath,
And, dry with grief, was turn'd into a stone,
Had not such passions in her head as I.
Methinks, that town there should be Troy, yon Ida's hill,
There Xanthus' stream, because here's Priamus,
And when I know it is not, then I die.   .

' *Acha.* And in this humour is Achates too;
I cannot choose but fall upon my knees,
And kiss his hand; O, where is Hecuba?
Here she was wont to sit, but saving air
Is nothing here; and what is this but stone?

Æn. O, yet this stone doth make Æneas weep;
And, would my prayers (as Pygmalion's did)
Could give it life, that under his conduct
We might sail back to Troy, and be reveng'd
On these hard-hearted Grecians, which rejoice
That nothing now is left of Priamus!
Oh, Priamus is left, and this is he
Come, come aboard; pursue the hateful Greeks.

Acha. What means Æneas?

Æn. Achates, though mine eyes say this is stone,
Yet thinks my mind that this is Priamus,
And when my grieved heart sighs and says no,
Then would it leap out to give Priam life.
O were I not at all, so thou might'st be!
Achates, see, King Priam wags his hand;
He is alive; Troy is not overcome!

Acha. Thy mind, Æneas, that would have it so,

Deludes thy eye-sight; Priamus is dead.

Æn. Ah, Troy is sack'd, and Priamus is dead;
And why should poor Æneas be alive?

Asca. Sweet father, leave to weep, this is not he:
For were it Priam, he would smile on me.

Acha. Æneas, see, here come the citizens;
Leave to lament, lest they laugh at our fears.

Enter CLOANTHUS, SERGESTUS, *and* ILIONEUS.

Æn. Lords of this town, or whatsoever style
Belongs unto your name, vouchsafe of ruth
To tell us who inhabits this fair town,
What kind of people, and who governs them:
For we are strangers driv'n on this shore,
And scarcely know within what clime we are.

Ilio. I hear Æneas' voice, but see him not,
For none of these can be our general.

Acha. Like Ilioneus speaks this nobleman,
But Ilioneus goes not in such robes.

Serg. You are Achates, or I deceiv'd.

Acha. Æneas, see Sergestus, or his ghost.

Ilio. He names Æneas; let us kiss his feet.

Cloan. It is our captain, see Ascanius.

Serg. Live long Æneas and Ascanius!

Æn. Achates, speak, for I am overjoy'd.

Acha. O, Ilioneus, art thou yet alive?

Ilio. Blest be the time I see Achates' face.

Cloan. Why turns Æneas from his trusty friends?

Æn. Sergestus, Ilioneus, and the rest,
Your sight amaz'd me: O, what destinies

Have brought my sweet companions in such plight?
O, tell me, for I long to be resolv'd.

Ilio. Lovely Æneas, these are Carthage walls,
And here Queen Dido wears th' imperial crown;
Who, for Troy's sake, hath entertain'd us all,
And clad us in these wealthy robes we wear.
Oft hath she ask'd us under whom we serv'd,
And when we told her, she would weep for grief,
Thinking the sea had swallow'd up thy ships;
And now she sees thee, how will she rejoice.

Serg. See, where her servitors pass through the hall
Bearing a banquet; Dido is not far.

Ilio. Look where she comes: Æneas, view her well

Æn. Well may I view her, but she sees not me.

Enter DIDO *and her Train.*

Dido. What stranger art thou, that dost eye me thus?

Æn. Sometime I was a Trojan, mighty queen:
But Troy is not;—what shall I say I am?

Ilio. Renowned Dido, 'tis our general, warlike Æneas.

Dido. Warlike Æneas! and in these base robes?
Go, fetch the garment which Sicheus wore:
Brave prince, welcome to Carthage and to me!
Both happy that Æneas is our guest:
Sit in this chair, and banquet with a queen;
Æneas is Æneas, were he clad
In weeds as bad as ever Irus wore.

Æn. This is no seat for one that's comfortless:
May it please your grace to let Æneas wait;
For though my birth be great, my fortune's mean,

Too mean to be companion to a queen.

Dido. Thy fortune may be greater than thy birth :
Sit down, Æneas, sit in Dido's place,
And if this be thy son, as I suppose,
Here let him sit ; be merry, lovely child.

Æn. This place beseems me not ; O, pardon me.

Dido. I'll have it so ; Æneas, be content.

Asca. Madam, you shall be my mother.

Dido. And so I will, sweet child : be merry, man,
Here's to thy better fortune and good stars.

Æn. In all humility, I thank your grace.

Dido. Remember who thou art, speak like thyself ;
Humility belongs to common grooms.

Æn. And who so miserable as Æneas is ?

Dido. Lies it in Dido's hands to make thee blest ?
Then be assur'd thou art not miserable.

Æn. O Priamus, O Troy, O Hecuba !

Dido. May I entreat thee to discourse at large,
And truly too, how Troy was overcome ?
For many tales go of that city's fall,
And scarcely do agree upon one point :
Some say Antenor did betray the town ;
Others report 'twas Sinon's perjury ;
But all in this, that Troy is overcome,
And Priam dead ; yet how, we hear no news.

Æn. A woeful tale bids Dido to unfold,
Whose memory, like pale death's stony mace,
Beats forth my senses from this troubled soul,
And makes Æneas sink at Dido's feet.

Dido. What! faints Æneas to remember Troy,

In whose defence he fought so valiantly?
Look up, and speak.

Æn. Then speak, Æneas, with Achilles' tongue!
And Dido, and you Carthagenian peers,
Hear me! but yet with Myrmidons' harsh ears,
Daily inur'd to broils and massacres,
Lest you be mov'd too much with my sad tale.
The Grecian soldiers, tir'd with ten years' war,
Began to cry, " Let us unto our ships,
Troy is invincible, why stay we here?"
With whose outcries Atrides being appall'd,
Summon'd the captains to his princely tent;
Who, looking on the scars we Trojans gave,
Seeing the number of their men decreas'd,
And the remainder weak, and out of heart,
Gave up their voices to dislodge the camp,
And so in troops all march'd to Tenedos;
Where, when they came, Ulysses on the sand
Assay'd with honey words to turn them back.
And as he spoke, to further his intent,
The winds did drive huge billows to the shore,
And heaven was darken'd with tempestuous clouds.
Then he alleg'd the gods would have them stay,
And prophecied Troy should be overcome:
And therewithal he call'd false Sinon forth,
A man compact of craft and perjury,
Whose 'ticing tongue was made of Hermes' pipe,
To force a hundred watchful eyes to sleep:
And him, Epeus having made the horse,
With sacrificing wreaths upon his head,

Ulysses sent to our unhappy town,
Who, grov'ling in the mire of Zanthus' banks,
His hands bound at his back, and both his eyes
Turn'd up to heaven, as one resolv'd to die,
Our Phrygian shepherds hal'd within the gates,
And brought unto the court of Priamus ;
To whom he us'd action so pitiful,
Looks so remorseful, vows so forcible,
As therewithal the old man, overcome,
Kiss'd him, embrac'd him, and unloos'd his bands,
And then,—O Dido, pardon me.

    Dido. Nay, leave not here ; resolve me of the rest.

    Æn. Oh ! the enchanting words of that base slave,
Made him to think Epeus' pine-tree horse
A sacrifice t' appease Minerva's wrath ;
The rather, for that one Laocoon,
Breaking a spear upon his hollow breast,
Was with two winged serpents stung to death.
Whereat, aghast, we were commanded straight,
With reverence, to draw it into Troy ;
In which unhappy work was I employ'd :
These hands did help to hale it to the gates,
Through which it could not enter, 'twas so huge.
O, had it never enter'd, Troy had stood.
But Priamus, impatient of delay,
Enforc'd a wide breach in that rampir'd wall,
Which thousand battering rams could never pierce,
And so came in this fatal instrument ·
At whose accursed feet, as overjoy'd,
We banqueted, till, overcome with wine,

Some surfeited, and others soundly slept.
Which Sinon viewing, caus'd the Greekish spies
To haste to Tenedos, and tell the camp :
Then he unlock'd the horse, and suddenly
From out his entrails, Neoptolemus,
Setting his spear upon the ground, leapt forth,
And after him a thousand Grecians more,
In whose stern faces shin'd the quenchless fire,
That after burnt the pride of Asia.
By this the camp was come unto the walls,
And through the breach did march into the streets,
Where, meeting with the rest, " kill! kill!" they cry'd.
Frighted with this confused noise, I rose,
And looking from a turret, might behold
Young infants swimming in their parents' blood!
Headless carcases piled up in heaps!
Virgins, half dead, dragg'd by their golden hair,
And with main force flung on a ring of pikes!
Old men with swords thrust through their aged sides,
Kneeling for mercy to a Greekish lad,
Who, with steel pole-axes, dash'd out their brains.
Then buckled I mine armour, drew my sword,
And thinking to go down, came Hector's ghost,
With ashy visage, blueish sulphur eyes,
His arms torn from his shoulders, and his breast
Furrow'd with wound, and, that which made me weep,
Thongs at his heels, by which Achilles' horse
Drew him in triumph through the Greekish camp,
Burst from the earth, crying, " Æneas, fly,
Troy is a-fire ! the Grecians have the town!"

Dido. O, Hector! who weeps not to hear thy name?

Æn. Yet flung I forth, and, desp'rate of my life,
Ran in the thickest throngs, and, with this sword,
Sent many of their savage ghosts to hell.
At last came Pyrrhus, fell and full of ire,
His harness dropping blood, and on his spear
The mangled head of Priam's youngest son;
And, after him, his band of Myrmidons,
With balls of wild-fire in their murd'ring paws,
Which made the funeral-flame that burnt fair Troy;
All which hemm'd me about, crying, This is he!

    Dido. Ha! how could poor Æneas 'scape their hands?

    Æn. My mother, Venus, jealous of my health,
Convey'd me from their crooked nets and bands;
So I escap'd the furious Pyrrhus' wrath:
Who then ran to the palace of the king,
And, at Jove's altar, finding Priamus,
About whose wither'd neck hung Hecuba,
Folding his hand in her's, and jointly both
Beating their breasts, and falling on the ground,
He with his faulchion's point rais'd up at once,
And with Megara's eyes star'd in their face,
Threat'ning a thousand deaths at every glance;
To whom the aged king thus trembling spoke:—
"Achilles' son, remember what I was,
Father of fifty sons, but they are slain;
Lord of my fortune, but my fortune's turn'd!
King of this city, but my Troy is fir'd!
And now am neither father, lord, nor king!
Yet who so wretched but desires to live?

O, let me live, great Neoptolemus!"
Not mov'd at all, but smiling at his tears,
This butcher, whilst his hands were yet held up,
Treading upon his breast, struck off his hands

    Dido. O end, Æneas, I can hear no more.

    Æn. At which the frantic queen leap'd on his face,
And in his eyelids hanging by the nails,
A little while prolong'd her husband's life.
At last, the soldiers pull'd her by the heels,
And swung her howling in the empty air,
Which sent an echo to the wounded king:
Whereat, he lifted up his bed-rid limbs,
And would have grappled with Achilles' son,
Forgetting both his want of strength and hands;
Which he, disdaining, whisk'd his sword about,
And with the wound thereof the king fell down;
Then from the navel to the throat at once
He ripp'd old Priam, at whose latter gasp,
Jove's marble statue 'gan to bend the brow,
As loathing Pyrrhus for this wicked act.
Yet he, undaunted, took his father's flag,
And dipp'd it in the old king's chill-cold blood,
And then in triumph ran into the streets,
Through which he could not pass for slaughter'd men;
So, leaning on his sword, he stood stone still,
Viewing the fire wherewith rich Ilion burnt.
By this, I got my father on my back,
This young boy in mine arms, and by the hand
Led fair Creusa, my beloved wife;
When thou, Achates, with thy sword mad'st way

And we were round environ'd with the Greeks,
O there I lost my wife! and had not we
Fought manfully, I had not told this tale.
Yet manhood would not serve; of force we fled;
And as we went unto our ships, thou know'st
We saw Cassandra sprawling in the streets,
Whom Ajax ravish'd in Diana's fane,
Her cheeks swoln with sighs, her hair all rent,
Whom I took up to bear unto our ships;
But suddenly the Grecians follow'd us,
And I, alas! was forc'd to let her lie.
Then got we to our ships, and, being aboard,
Polyxena cried out, Æneas! stay!
The Greeks pursue me! stay, and take me in!
Mov'd with her voice, I leap'd into the sea,
Thinking to bear her on my back aboard,
For all our ships were launch'd into the deep,
And, as I swam, she, standing on the shore,
Was by the cruel Myrmidons surpris'd,
And after by that Pyrrhus sacrific'd.

   Dido. I die with melting ruth; Æneas, leave!
   Anna. O what became of aged Hecuba?
   Iar. How got Æneas to the fleet again?
   Dido. But how 'scaped Helen, she that caused this war?
   Æn. Achates, speak, sorrow hath tir'd me quite.
   Acha. What happen'd to the queen we cannot shew;
We hear they led her captive into Greece:
As for Æneas, he swam quickly back,
And Helena betray'd Deiphobus,
Her lover, after Alexander died,

And so was reconcil'd to Menelaus.

    Dido. O, had that 'ticing strumpet ne'er been born!
Trojan, thy ruthful tale hath made me sad.
Come, let us think upon some pleasing sport,
To rid me from these melancholy thoughts. [*exeunt omnes.*

   Enter Venus *and* Cupid, Venus *takes* Ascanius *by the sleeve*

    Ven. Fair child, stay thou with Dido's waiting maid;
I'll give thee sugar-almonds, sweet conserves,
A silver girdle, and a golden purse,
And this young prince shall be thy playfellow.

    Asc. Are you Queen Dido's son?

    Cup. Aye, and my mother gave me this fine bow.

    Asc. Shall I have such a quiver and a bow?

    Ven. Such bow, such quiver, and such golden shafts,
Will Dido give to sweet Ascanius.
For Dido's sake I take thee in my arms,
And stick these spangled feathers in thy hat;
Eat comfits in mine arms, and I will sing
Now is he fast asleep, and in this grove,
Amongst green brakes I'll lay Ascanius,
And strew him with sweet-smelling violets,
Blushing roses, purple hyacinth:
These milk-white doves shall be his sentinels,
Who, if that any seek to do him hurt,
Will quickly fly to Cytherea's fist.
Now, Cupid, turn thee to Ascanius' shape,
And go to Dido, who, instead of him,
Will set thee on her lap, and play with thee;
Then touch her white breast with this arrow head,

That she may dote upon Æneas' love,
And by that means repair his broken ships,
Victual his soldiers, give him wealthy gifts,
And he, at last, depart to Italy,
Or else in Carthage make his kingly throne.

Cup. I will, fair mother, and so play my part
As every touch shall wound Queen Dido's heart.

Ven. Sleep, my sweet nephew, in these cooling shades,
Free from the murmur of these running streams,
The cry of beasts, the rattling of the winds,
Or whisking of these leaves; all shall be still,
And nothing interrupt thy quiet sleep,
Till I return and take thee hence again.   [*exeunt.*

ACT III.   SCENE I.

Enter CUPID.

Cup. Now, Cupid, cause the Carthaginian queen
To be enamour'd of thy brother's looks.
Convey this golden arrow in thy sleeve,
Lest she imagine thou art Venus' son;
And when she strokes thee softly on the head,
Then shall I touch her breast and conquer her.

Enter IARBAS, ANNA, *and* DIDO.

Iar. How long, fair Dido, shall I pine for thee?
'Tis not enough that thou dost grant me love,

But that I may enjoy what I desire :
That love is childish which consists in words.

Dido. Iarbas, know, that thou, of all my wooers,
And yet have I had many mightier kings,
Hast had the greatest favours I could give.
I fear me, Dido hath been counted light,
In being too familiar with Iarbas ;
Albeit the gods do know, no wanton thought
Had ever residence in Dido's breast.

Iar. But Dido is the favour I request.

Dido. Fear not, Iarbas, Dido may be thine.

Anna. Look, sister, how Æneas' little son
Plays with your garments and embraceth you.

Cup. No, Dido will not take me in her arms.
I shall not be her son, she loves me not.

Dido. Weep not, sweet boy, thou shalt be Dido's son ;
Sit in my lap, and let me hear thee sing.   [*Cupid sings.*
No more, my child, now talk another while,
And tell me where learn'st thou this pretty song.

Cup. My cousin Helen taught it me in Troy.

Dido. How lovely is Ascanius when he smiles !

Cup. Will Dido let me hang about her neck ?

Dido. Aye, wag, and give thee leave to kiss her too.

Cup. What will you give me ? Now, I'll have this fan.

Dido. Take it, Ascanius, for thy father's sake.

Iar Come, Dido, leave Ascanius, let us walk.

Dido. Go thou away, Ascanius shall stay.

Iar. Ungentle queen ! is this thy love to me ?

Dido. O stay, Iarbas, and I'll go with thee.

Cup. And if my mother go, I'll follow her.

Dido Why stay'st thou here? thou art no love of mine!

Iar. Iarbas, die, seeing she abandons thee.

Dido. No; live Iarbas: what hast thou deserv'd,
That I should say thou art no love of mine?
Something thou hast deserv'd. Away, I say;
Depart from Carthage—come not in my sight.

Iar. Am I not king of rich Getulia?

Dido Iarbas, pardon me, and stay awhile.

Cup. Mother, look here.

Dido. What tell'st thou me of rich Getulia?
Am not I queen of Lybia? then depart.

Iar. I'go to feed the humour of my love,
Yet not from Carthage for a thousand worlds.

Dido. Iarbas!

Iar. Doth Dido call me back?

Dido. No; but I charge thee never look on me.

Iar. Then pull out both mine eyes, or let me die.

[*exit Iarbas.*

Anna. Wherefore doth Dido bid Iarbas go?

Dido. Because his loathsome sight offends mine eye,
And in my thoughts is shrin'd another Jove.
O Anna! didst thou know how sweet love were,
Full soon would'st thou abjure this single life.

Anna. Poor soul! I know too well the power of love.
O that Iarbas could but fancy me!

Dido. Is not Æneas fair and beautiful?

Anna. Yes, and Iarbas foul and favourless.

Dido. Is he not eloquent in all his speech?

Anna. Yes, and Iarbas rude and rustical

Dido. Name not Iarbas, but, sweet Anna, say,

Is not Æneas worthy Dido's love?

   Anna. O sister! were you empress of the world,
Æneas well deserves to be your love.
So lovely is he, that, where'er he goes,
The people swarm to gaze him in the face.

   Dido. But tell them, none shall gaze on him but I,
Lest their gross eye-beams taint my lover's cheeks.
Anna, good sister Anna, go for him,
Lest with these sweet thoughts I melt clean away.

   Anna. Then, sister, you'll abjure Iarbas' love?

   Dido. Yet must I hear that loathsome name again?
Run for Æneas, or I'll fly to him.   [*exit Anna.*

   Cup. You shall not hurt my father when he comes.

   Dido. No, for thy sake, I'll love thy father well.
O dull-conceited Dido! that till now
Didst never think Æneas beautiful!
But now, for quittance of this oversight,
I'll make me bracelets of his golden hair;
His glist'ring eyes shall be my looking-glass,
His lips an altar, where I'll offer up
As many kisses as the sea hath sands.
Instead of music I will hear him speak,—
His looks shall be my only library,—
And thou, Æneas, Dido's treasury,
In whose fair bosom I will lock more wealth
Than twenty thousand Indias can afford.
O here he comes: Love, love, give Dido leave
To be more modest than her thoughts admit,
Lest I be made a wonder to the world.

Enter ÆNEAS, ACHATES, SERGESTUS, ILIONEUS, *and* CLOANTHUS.

Achates, how doth Carthage please your lord?

Acha. That will Æneas shew your majesty.

Dido. Æneas, art thou there?

Æn. I understand your highness sent for me.

Dido. No; but now thou art here, tell me in sooth
In what might Dido highly pleasure thee.

Æn. So much have I receiv'd at Dido's hands,
As, without blushing, I can ask no more:
Yet, queen of Afric, are my ships unrigg'd,
My sails all rent in sunder with the wind,
My oars broken, and my tackling lost,
Yea, all my navy split with rocks and shelves;
Nor stern nor anchor have our maimed fleet;
Our masts the furious winds struck overboard:
Which piteous wants if Dido will supply,
We will account her author of our lives.

Dido. Æneas, I'll repair thy Trojan ships,
Conditionally that thou wilt stay with me,
And let Achates sail to Italy:
I'll give thee tackling made of riveld gold,
Wound on the barks of odoriferous trees,
Oars of massy ivory, full of holes,
Through which the water shall delight to play;
Thy anchors shall be hew'd from crystal rocks,
Which, if thou lose, shall shine above the waves;
The masts, whereon thy swelling sails shall hang,
Hollow pyramids of silver plate;
The sails of folded lawn, where shall be wrought
The wars of Troy, but not Troy's overthrow;

For ballast, empty Dido's treasury:
Take what ye will, but leave Æneas here.
Achates, thou shalt be so meanly clad,
As sea-born nymphs shall swarm about thy ships,
And wanton mermaids court thee with sweet songs,
Flinging in favours of more sovereign worth
Than Thetis hangs about Apollo's neck,
So that Æneas may but stay with me.

    Æn. Wherefore would Dido have Æneas stay?

    Dido. To war against my bordering enemies.
Æneas, think not Dido is in love;
For if that any man could conquer me,
I had been wedded ere Æneas came:
See where the pictures of my suitors hang;
And are not these as fair as fair may be?

    Acha. I saw this man at Troy, ere Troy was sack'd.

    Æn. I this in Greece, when Paris stole fair Helen.

    Ilio. This man and I were at Olympus' games.

    Serg. I know this face; he is a Persian born:
I travell'd with him to Ætolia.

    Cloan. And I in Athens, with this gentleman,
Unless I be deceiv'd, disputed once.

    Dido. But speak, Æneas; know you none of these?

    Æn. No, madam; but it seems that these are kings.

    Dido. All these, and others which I never saw,
Have been most urgent suitors for my love;
Some came in person, others sent their legates,
Yet none obtain'd me: I am free from all;
And yet, God knows, entangled unto one.
This was an orator, and thought, by words,

To compass me; but yet he was deceiv'd:
And this a Spartan courtier, vain and wild;
But his fantastic humours pleas'd not me:
This was Alcion, a musician;
But, play'd he ne'er so sweet, I let him go:
This was the wealthy king of Thessaly;
But I had gold enough, and cast him off:
This, Meleager's son, a warlike prince;
But weapons 'gree not with my tender years:
The rest are such as all the world well knows;
Yet here I swear, by heaven and him I love,
I was as far from love as they from hate.

   Æn. O happy shall he be whom Dido loves!

   Dido. Then never say that thou art miserable:
Because, it may be, thou shalt be my love:
Yet boast not of it, for I love thee not,
And yet I hate thee not Oh, if I speak
I shall betray myself: Æneas, speak;
We two will go a hunting in the woods;
But not so much for thee,—thou art but one,—
As for Achates, and his followers.   *[exeunt.*

SCENE II.

Enter JUNO *to* ASCANIUS, *asleep.*

   Juno. Here lies my hate, Æneas' cursed brat,
The boy wherein false destiny delights,
The heir of Fury, the favourite of the Fates,
That ugly imp that shall outwear my wrath,
And wrong my deity with high disgrace:
But I will take another order now,

And raze th' eternal register of time.
Troy shall no more call him her second hope,
Nor Venus triumph in his tender youth ;
For here, in spite of heav'n, I'll murder him,
And feed infection with his let-out life :
Say, Paris, now shall Venus have the ball ?
Say, vengeance, now shall her Ascanius die ?
O no, God wot, I cannot watch my time,
Nor quit good turns with double fee down told.
Tut ! I am simple without might to hurt,
And have no gall at all to grieve my foes ;
But lustful Jove, and his adulterous child,
Shall find it written on confusion's front,
That only Juno rules in Rhamnus town.

Enter VENUS.

   Ven What should this mean? my doves are back
        return'd,
Who warn me of such danger prest at hand,
To harm my sweet Ascanius' lovely life.
Juno, my mortal foe, what make you here ?
Avaunt, old witch! and trouble not my wits.

   Juno. Fie, Venus! that such causeless words of wrath,
Should e'er defile so fair a mouth as thine.
Are not we both sprung of celestial race,
And banquet, as two sisters, with the gods?
Why is it, then, displeasure should disjoin,
Whom kindred and acquaintance co-unites ?

   Ven. Out, hateful hag! thou would'st have slain my
        son,

Had not my doves discover'd thy intent;
But I will tear thy eyes from forth thy head,
And feast the birds with their blood-shotten balls,
If thou but lay thy fingers on my boy!

Juno. Is this, then, all the thanks that I shall have,
For saving him from snakes and serpents' stings,
That would have kill'd him, sleeping, as he lay?
What, though I was offended with thy son,
And wrought him mickle woe on sea and land,
When, for the hate of Trojan Ganymede,
That was advanced by my Hebe's shame,
And Paris' judgment of the heavenly ball,
I muster'd all the winds unto his wreck,
And urg'd each element to his annoy:
Yet now I do repent me of his ruth,
And wish that I had never wrong'd him so.
Bootless, I saw, it was to war with fate,
That hath so many unresisted friends:
Wherefore I change my counsel with the time,
And planted love where envy erst had sprung.

Ven. Sister of Jove! if that thy love be such
As these thy protestations do paint forth,
We two, as friends, one fortune will divide:
Cupid shall lay his arrows in thy lap,
And, to a sceptre, change his golden shafts;
Fancy and modesty shall live as mates;
And thy fair peacocks by my pigeons perch:
Love my Æneas, and desire is thine;
The day, the night, my swans, my sweets, are thi

Juno. More than melodious are these words to me,

That overcloy my soul with their content:
Venus, sweet Venus! how may I deserve
Such amorous favours at thy beauteous hand?
But, that thou may'st more easily perceive
How highly I do prize this amity,
Hark to a motion of eternal league,
Which I will make in quittance of thy love
Thy son, thou know'st, with Dido now remains,
And feeds his eyes with favours of her court;
She, likewise, in admiring spends her time,
And cannot talk, nor think, of aught but him.
Why should not they then join in marriage,
And bring forth mighty kings to Carthage town,
Whom casualty of sea hath made such friends?
And, Venus, let there be a match confirm'd
Betwixt these two, whose loves are so alike;
And both our deities, conjoin'd in one,
Shall chain felicity unto their throne.

    Ven. Well could I like this reconcilement's means;
But, much I fear, my son will ne'er consent;
Whose armed soul, already on the sea,
Darts forth her light to Lavinia's shore.

    Juno Fair queen of love! I will divorce these doubts,
And find the way to weary such fond thoughts.
This day they both a hunting forth will ride
Into these woods, adjoining to these walls;
When, in the midst of all their gamesome sports,
I'll make the clouds dissolve their wat'ry works,
And drench Silvanus' dwellings with their showers;
Then, in one cave, the queen and he shall meet,

Ven. Sister, I see you savour of my wiles:
Be it as you will have it for this once.
Mean time, Ascanius shall be my charge;
Whom I will bear to Ida in mine arms,
And couch him in Adonis' purple down. [*exeunt.*

SCENE III.

Enter DIDO, ÆNEAS, ANNA, IARBAS, ACHATES, *and Followers*

Dido. Æneas, think not but I honour thee,
That thus in person go with thee to hunt:
My princely robes, thou see'st, are laid aside,
Whose glittering pomp Diana's shroud supplies.
All fellows now, dispos'd alike to sport;
The woods are wide, and we have store of game.
Fair Trojan, hold my golden bow awhile,
Until I gird my quiver to my side:
Lords, go before; we two must talk alone.

Iar. Ungentle! can she wrong Iarbas so?
I'll die before a stranger have that grace.
We two will talk alone;—what words be these?

Dido. What makes Iarbas here of all the rest?
We would have gone without your company.

Æn. But love and duty led him on perhaps,
To press beyond acceptance to your sight.

Iar. Why, man of Troy, do I offend thine eyes?
Or art thou griev'd thy betters press so nigh?

Dido. How now, Gætulian! are ye grown so brave,
To challenge us with your comparisons?
Peasant! go seek companions like thyself,
And meddle not with any that I love:

D

Æneas, be not mov'd at what he says;
For, otherwise, he will be out of joint.

Iar. Women may wrong, by privilege of love ;
But, should that man of men, Dido except,
Have taunted me in these opprobrious terms,
I would have either drunk his dying blood,
Or else I would have given my life in gage.

Dido. Huntsmen, why pitch you not your toils apace,
And rouse the light-foot deer from forth their lair?

Anna. Sister, see ! see Ascanius in his pomp,
Bearing his hunt-spear bravely in his hand.

Dido. Yea, little son, are you so forward now?

Asc. Aye, mother; I shall one day be a man,
And better able unto other arms;
Mean time, these wanton weapons serve my war,
Which I will break betwixt a lion's jaws.

Dido. What! dar'st thou look a lion in the face?

Asc. Aye, and outface him too, do what he can.

Anna. How like his father speaketh he in all.

Æn. And might I live to see him sack rich Thebes,
And load his spear with Grecian princes' heads,
Then would I wish me with Anchises' tomb,
And dead to honour that hath brought me up.

Iar. And might I live to see thee shipp'd away,
And hoist aloft on Neptune's hideous hills,
Then would I wish me in fair Dido's arms,
And dead to scorn that hath pursued me so.

Æn. Stout friend Achates, do'st thou know this wood?

Acha. As I remember, here you shot the deer
That sav'd your famish'd soldiers' lives from death,

When first you set your foot upon the shore;
And here we met fair Venus, virgin like,
Bearing her bow and quiver at her back.

Æn. O how these irksome labours now delight
And overjoy my thoughts with their escape!
Who would not undergo all kind of toil,
To be well stor'd with such a winter's tale?

Dido. Æneas, leave these dumps, and let's away,
Some to the mountains, some unto the soil,
You to the vallies, thou unto the house.

[exeunt all but Iarbas.

Iar. Aye, this it is which wounds me to the death,
To see a Phrygian, far set to the sea,
Prefer'd before a man of majesty.
O love! O hate! O cruel women's hearts,
That imitate the moon in every change!
And, like the planets, ever love to range:
What shall I do, thus wronged with disdain,
Revenge me on Æneas, or on her?
On her? fond man! that were to war 'gainst heaven,
And with one shaft provoke ten thousand darts:
This Trojan's end will be thy envy's aim,
Whose blood will reconcile thee to content,
And make love drunken with thy sweet desire;
But Dido, that now holdeth him so dear,
Will die with very tidings of his death:
But time will discontinue her content,
And mould her mind unto new fancies' shapes.
O, God of heaven! turn the hand of fate
Unto that happy day of my delight;

And then,—what then?—Iarbas shall but love;
So doth he now, though not with equal gain,
That resteth in the rival of thy pain,
Who ne'er will cease to soar till he be slain.   [*exit*

SCENE IV.

A Storm.—Enter ÆNEAS *and* DIDO *in the cave, at several times.*

Dido. Æneas!

Æn. Dido!

Dido Tell me, dear love! how found you out this
          cave?

Æn. By chance, sweet queen! as Mars and Venus met.

Dido. Why, that was in a net, here we are loose;
And yet, I am not free; oh, would I were!

Æn. Why, what is that Dido may desire,
And not obtain, be it in human power?

Dido. The thing that I will die before I ask,
And yet desire to have before I die.

Æn. It is not aught Æneas may achieve?

Dido. Æneas, no; although his eyes do pierce.

Æn. What, hath Iarbas anger'd her in aught?
And will she be avenged on his life?

Dido. Not anger'd me, except in ang'ring thee.

Æn. Who then, of all so cruel, may he be,
That should detain thine eye in his defects?

Dido. The man that I do eye where'er I am;
Whose amorous face, like Pæan's, sparkles fire,
When as he butts his beams on Flora's bed.
Prometheus hath put on Cupid's shape,
And I must perish in his burning arms:

Æneas, O Æneas! quench these flames.

Æn. What ails my queen? Is she fall'n sick of late?

Dido. Not sick, my love, but sick: I must conceal
The torment that it boots me not reveal;
And yet I'll speak, and yet I'll hold my peace:
Do shame her worst, I will disclose my grief:
Æneas, thou art he! what did I say?
Something it was that now I have forgot.

Æn. What means fair Dido by this doubtful speech?

Dido. Nay, nothing, but Æneas loves me not.

Æn. Æneas' thoughts dare not ascend so high
As Dido's heart, which monarchs might not scale.

Dido. It was because I saw no king like thee,
Whose golden crown might balance my content;
But now, that I have found what to affect,
I follow one that loveth fame for me,
And rather had seen fair Sirens' eyes,
Than to the Carthage queen, that dies for him.

Æn. If that your majesty can look so low
As my despised worths, that shun all praise,
With this my hand I give to you my heart,
And vow, by all the gods of hospitality,
By heaven and earth, and my fair brother's bow,
By Paphos, Capys, and the purple sea,
From whence my radiant mother did descend,
And by this sword, that saved me from the Greeks,
Never to leave these new upreared walls,
While Dido lives and rules in Juno's town,—
Never to like or love any but her.

Dido. What more than Delian music do I hear,

That calls my soul from forth his living seat
To move unto the measures of delight?
Kind clouds that sent forth such a courteous storm,
As made disdain to fly to fancy's lap:
Stout love, in mine arms make thy Italy,
Whose crown and kingdom rest at thy command:
Sichæus, not Æneas, be thou call'd;
The King of Carthage, not Anchises' son.
Hold; take these jewels at thy lover's hand,
These golden bracelets, and this wedding ring,
Wherewith my husband woo'd me yet a maid,
And be thou king of Lybia by my gift.

                              [*exeunt to the cave.*

ACT IV. SCENE I.

Enter ACHATES, CUPID *as Ascanius,* IARBAS, *and* ANNA.

Acha. Did ever men see such a sudden storm?
Or day so clear, so suddenly o'ercast?

Iar. I think, some fell enchantress dwelleth here,
That can call them forth when as she please,
And dive into black tempests' treasury,
When as she means to mask the world with clouds.

Anna. In all my life I never knew the like;
It hail'd, it snow'd, it lighten'd, all at once.

Acha. I think, it was the devil's rev'lling night,
There was such hurly-burly in the heavens:
Doubtless, Apollo's axle-tree is crack'd,
Or aged Atlas' shoulder out of joint,

The motion was so over violent.

   Iar. In all this coil, where have ye left the queen?

   Asca. Nay, where's my warlike father, can you tell?

   Anna. Behold, where both of them come forth the cave.

   Iar. Come forth the cave! can heaven endure the
       sight?

Iarbas, curse that unrevenging Jove,

Whose flinty darts slept in Tiphœus' den,

While these adult'rers surfeited with sin:

Nature, why mad'st me not some pois'nous beast,

That, with the sharpness of my edged sting,

I might have stak'd them both unto the earth,

Whilst they were sporting in this darksome cave?

Enter ÆNEAS *and* DIDO

   Æn. The air is clear, and southern winds are whist;

Come, Dido, let us hasten to the town,

Since gloomy Æolus doth cease to frown.

   Dido. Achates and Ascanius, well met.

   Æn. Fair Anna! how escap'd you from the shower?

   Anna. As others did,—by running to the wood.

   Dido. But where were you, Iarbas, all this while?

   Iar. Not with Æneas in the ugly cave.

   Dido. I see, Æneas sticketh in your mind;

But I will soon put by that stumbling block,

And quell those hopes that thus employ your cares.

[*exeunt.*

SCENE II.

Enter IARBAS, *to sacrifice.*

   Iar. Come, servants, come; bring forth the sacrifice,

That I may pacify that gloomy Jove,
Whose empty altars have enlarg'd our ills.
Eternal Jove! great master of the clouds!
Father of gladness, and all frolic thoughts!
That with thy gloomy hand corrects the heaven,
When airy creatures war amongst themselves;
Hear, hear, O hear! Iarbas' plaining prayers,
Whose hideous echoes make the welkin howl,
And all the woods Eliza to resound:
The woman that thou will'd us entertain,
Where, straying in our borders up and down,
She crav'd a hide of ground to build a town,
With whom we did divide both laws and land,
And all the fruits that plenty else sends forth,
Scorning our loves and royal marriage rites,
Yields up her beauty to a stranger's bed;
Who, having wrought her shame, is straight-way fled:
Now, if thou be'st a pitying god of power,
On whom ruth and compassion ever waits,
Redress these wrongs, and warn him to his ships,
That now afflicts me with his flattering eyes.

Enter ANNA.

   Anna. How now, Iarbas; at your prayers so hard?
   Iar. Aye, Anna: is there aught you would with me?
   Anna. Nay, no such weighty business of import,
But may be slack'd until another time;
Yet, if you would partake with me the cause
Of this devotion that detaineth you,
I would be thankful for such courtesy.

Iar. Anna, against this Trojan do I pray,
Who seeks to rob me of thy sister's love,
And dive into her heart by colour'd looks.

Anna. Alas, poor king! that labours so in vain,
For her that so delighteth in thy pain :
Be rul'd by me, and seek some other love,
Whose yielding heart may yield thee more relief.

Iar. Mine eye is fix'd where fancy cannot start:
O leave me! leave me to my silent thoughts,
That register the number of my ruth,
And I will either move the thoughtless flint,
Or drop out both mine eyes in drizzling tears,
Before my sorrow's tide has any stint.

Anna I will not leave Iarbas, whom I love,
In this delight of dying pensiveness;
Away with Dido; Anna be thy song;
Anna, that doth admire thee more than heaven.

Iar. I may, nor will, list to such loathsome change,
That intercepts the course of my desire :
Servants, come, fetch these empty vessels here,
For I will fly from these alluring eyes,
That do pursue my peace where'er it goes.   [*exit*

Anna. Iarbas, stay ; loving Iarbas, stay,
For I have honey to present thee with.
Hard-hearted ! wilt not deign to hear me speak ?
I'll follow thee with outcries ne'ertheless,
And strew thy walks with my dishevell'd hair.   [*exit.*

SCENE III.

Enter ÆNEAS.

Æn. Carthage, my friendly host, adieu!
Since destiny doth call me from thy shore:
Hermes this night, descending in a dream,
Hath summon'd me to fruitful Italy;
Jove wills it so,—my mother wills it so:
Let my Phænissa grant, and then I go.
Grant she or no, Æneas must away;
Whose golden fortune, clogg'd with courtly ease,
Cannot ascend to fame's immortal house,
Or banquet in bright honour's burnish'd hall,
'Till he hath furrow'd Neptune's glassy fields,
And cut a passage through his topless hills.'
Achates, come forth; Sergestus, Ilioneus,
Cloanthus, haste away; Æneas calls.

Enter ACHATES, CLOANTHUS, SERGESTUS, *and* ILIONEUS

Acha. What wills our lord, or wherefore did he call?
Æn. The dream, brave mates, that did beset my bed,
When sleep but newly had embrac'd the night,
Commands me leave these unrenowned beams,
Whereas nobility abhors to stay,
And none but base Æneas will abide.
Aboard! aboard! since fates do bid aboard,
And slice the sea with sable-colour'd ships,
On whom the nimble winds may all day wait,
And follow them, as footmen, through the deep;

Yet Dido casts her eyes, like anchors, out,
To stay my fleet from loosing forth the bay:
' Come back, come back,' I hear her cry a-far,
' And let me link my body to thy lips,
That, tied together by the striving tongues,
We may, as one, sail into Italy.'

   Acha. Banish that 'ticing dame from forth your mouth,
And follow your fore-seeing star in all:
This is no life for men at arms to live,
Where dalliance doth consume a soldier's strength,
And wanton motions of alluring eyes
Effeminate our minds, inur'd to war.

   Ilio Why, let us build a city of our own,
And not stand ling'ring here for am'rous looks.
Will Dido raise old Priam forth his grave,
And build the town again the Greeks did burn?
No, no; she cares not how we sink or swim,
So she may have Æneas in her arms.

   Clo. To Italy, sweet friends! to Italy!
We will not stay a minute longer here.

   Æn. Trojans, aboard, and I will follow you:
I fain would go, yet beauty calls me back:
To leave her so, and not once say, farewell!
Were to transgress against all laws of love:
But, if I use such ceremonious thanks
As parting friends accustom on the shore,
Her silver arms will coil me round about,
And tears of pearl cry, ' stay, Æneas, stay;'
Each word she says will then contain a crown,
And every speech be ended with a kiss:

I may not dure this female drudgery;
To sea, Æneas, find out Italy.　　　　　　　　　[*exeunt*.

SCENE IV.

Enter DIDO *and* ANNA.

Dido. O, Anna, run unto the water-side;
They say Æneas' men are going a-board;
It may be he will steal away with them:
Stay not to answer me; run, Anna, run.
O, foolish Trojans, that would steal from hence,
And not let Dido understand their drift:
I would have given Achates store of gold,
And Ilioneus gum and Lybian spice;
The common soldiers rich embroider'd coats,
And silver whistles to controul the winds,
Which Circe sent Sichæus when he liv'd:
Unworthy are they of a queen's reward.
See, where they come, how might I do to chide?

Enter ANNA, *with* ÆNEAS, ACHATES, ILIONEUS, *and* SERGESTUS.

Anna. 'Twas time to run, Æneas had been gone;
The sails were hoisting up, and he aboard.
　Dido. Is this thy love to me?
　Æn. O, princely Dido, give me leave to speak;
I went to take my farewell of Achates.
　Dido. How haps Achates bid me not farewell?
　Acha. Because I fear'd your grace would keep me here.
　Dido. To rid thee of that doubt, aboard again;

I charge thee put to sea, and stay not here.

    Acha. Then let Æneas go aboard with us.

    Dido. Get you aboard, Æneas means to stay.

    Æn. The sea is rough, the wind blows to the shore.

    Dido. O, false Æneas, now the sea is rough,

But when you were aboard 'twas calm enough ;

Thou and Achates meant to sail away.

    Æn. Hath not the Carthage queen mine only son ?

Thinks Dido I will go and leave him here ?

    Dido. Æneas, pardon me, for I forgot

That young Ascanius lay with me this night ;

Love made me jealous ; but, to make amends,

Wear the imperial crown of Lybia,

Sway thou the Punick sceptre in my stead,

And punish me, Æneas, for this crime.

    Æn. This kiss shall be fair Dido's punishment.

    Dido. O, how a crown becomes Æneas' head !

Stay here, Æneas, and command as king.

    Æn. How vain am I to wear this diadem,

And bear this golden sceptre in my hand !

[*Aside.*] A burgonet of steel, and not a crown,

A sword, and not a sceptre, fits Æneas.

    Dido. O, keep them still, and let me gaze my fill.

Now looks Æneas like immortal Jove ;

O, where is Ganymede, to hold his cup,

And Mercury, to fly for what he calls ?

Ten thousand Cupids hover in the air,

And fan it in Æneas' lovely face :

O, that the clouds were here wherein thou fleest,

That thou and I unseen might sport ourselves ;

Heaven, envious of our joys, is waxen pale;
And when we whisper, then the stars fall down,
To be partakers of our honey talk.

Æn. O, Dido, patroness of all our lives,
When I leave thee, death be my punishment;
Swell, raging seas! frown, wayward destinies!
Blow, winds! threaten, ye rocks and sandy shelves!
This is the harbour that Æneas seeks.
Let's see what tempests can annoy me now.

Dido. Not all the world can take thee from mine arms;
Æneas may command as many Moors,
As in the sea are little water-drops.
And now, to make experience of my love,
Fair sister Anna, lead my lover forth,
And, seated on my gennet, let him ride
As Dido's husband through the Punic streets;
And will my guard, with Mauritanian darts,
To wait upon him as their sov'reign lord.

Anna. What if the citizens repine thereat?

Dido Those that dislike what Dido gives in charge,
Command my guard to slay for their offence.
Shall vulgar peasants storm at what I do?
The ground is mine that gives them sustenance,
The air wherein they breathe, the water, fire,
All that they have, their lands, their goods, their lives,
And I, the goddess of all these, command
Æneas ride as Carthaginian king.

Acha. Æneas, for his parentage, deserves
As large a kingdom as is Lybia.

Æn. Aye, and unless the destinies be false,

I shall be planted in as rich a land.

   Dido. Speak of no other land; this land is thine,
Dido is thine, henceforth I'll call thee lord:
Do as I bid thee, sister; lead the way,
And from a turret I'll behold my love.

   Æn. Then here in me shall flourish Priam's race,
And thou and I, Achates, for revenge,
For Troy, for Priam, for his fifty sons,
Our kinsmen's loves and thousand guiltless souls,
Will lead a host against the hateful Greeks,
And fire proud Lacedemon o'er their heads.   [*exit.*

   Dido. Speaks not Æneas like a conqueror?
O, blessed tempests that did drive him in,
O, happy sand that made him run aground;
Henceforth you shall be our Carthage gods.
Aye, but it may be he will leave my love,
And seek a foreign land, call'd Italy;
O, that I had a charm to keep the winds
Within the closure of a golden ball;
Or that the Tyrrhene sea were in mine arms,.
That he might suffer shipwreck on my breast,
As oft as he attempts to hoist up sail:
I must prevent him, wishing will not serve;
Go, bid my nurse take young Ascanius,
And bear him in the country to her house,
Æneas will not go without his son;
Yet, lest he should, for I am full of fear,
Bring me his oars, his tackling, and his sails.
What if I sink his ships? O, he will frown:
Better he frown, than I should die for grief.

I cannot see him frown, it may not be ;
Armies of foes resolv'd to win this town,
Or impious traitors vow'd to have my life,
Affright me not, only Æneas' frown
Is that which terrifies poor Dido's heàrt ;
Not bloody spears appearing in the air,
Presage the downfall of my empery,
Nor blazing comets threaten Dido's death ;
It is Æneas' frown that ends my days :
If he forsake me not, I never die ;
For in his looks I see eternity,
And he'll make me immortal with a kiss.

Enter a Lord.

Lord. Your nurse is gone with young Ascanius ;
And here's Æneas' tackling, oars, and sails.

Dido. Are these the sails that, in despite of me,
Pack'd with the winds to bear Æneas hence ?
I'll hang ye in the chamber where I lie ;
Drive if you can my house to Italy :
I'll set the casement open, that the winds
May enter in, and once again conspire
Against the life of me, poor Carthage queen ;
But though he go, he stays in Carthage still,
And let rich Carthage float upon the seas,
So I may have Æneas in mine arms.
Is this the wood that grew in Carthage plains,
And would be toiling in the wat'ry billows,
To rob their mistress of her Trojan guest ?
O, cursed tree, had'st thou but wit or sense,

To measure how I prize Æneas' love,
Thou would'st have leap'd from out the sailor's hands,
And told me that Æneas meant to go:
And yet I blame thee not, thou art but wood.
The water, which our poets term a nymph,
Why did it suffer thee to touch her breast,
And shrunk not back, knowing my love was there?
The water is an element, no nymph.
Why should I blame Æneas for his flight?
O, Dido, blame not him, but break his oars;
These were the instruments that launch'd him forth;
There's not so much as this base tackling too,
But dares to heap up sorrow to my heart.
Was it not you that hoisted up these sails?
Why burst you not, and they fell in the seas?
For this will Dido tie ye full of knots,
And shear ye all asunder with her hands;
Now serve to chastise shipboys for their faults,
Ye shall no more offend the Carthage queen.
Now, let him hang my favours on his masts,
And see if those will serve instead of sails;
For tackling, let him take the chains of gold,
Which I bestow'd upon his followers;
Instead of oars, let him use his hands,
And swim to Italy, I'll keep these sure:
Come, bear them in.   *[exeunt.*

SCENE V.

Enter the NURSE *with* CUPID, *as Ascanius.*

Nurse. My lord Ascanius, ye must go with me.

  Cup. Whither must I go? I'll stay with my mother.

  Nurse. No, thou shalt go with me unto my house.

I have an orchard that hath store of plums,

Brown almonds, servises, ripe figs, and dates,

Dewberries, apples, yellow oranges;

A garden where are bee-hives full of honey,

Musk-roses, and a thousand sorts of flowers;

And in the midst doth run a silver stream,

Where thou shalt see the red-gill'd fishes leap,

White swans, and many lovely water-fowls;

Now speak, Ascanius, will ye go or no?

    Cup. Come, come, I'll go, how far hence is your house?

    Nurse. But hereby, child, we shall get thither straight.

    Cup. Nurse, I am weary, will you carry me?

    Nurse Aye, so you'll dwell with me, and call me mother

    Cup. So you'll love me, I care not if I do.

    Nurse. That I might live to see this boy a man!

How prettily he laughs. Go, ye wag,

You'll be a twigger when you come to age.

Say Dido what she will, I am not old;

I'll be no more a widow, I am young,

I'll have a husband, or else a lover.

    Cup A husband and no teeth!

    Nurse. O, what mean I to have such foolish thoughts?

Foolish is love, a toy. O, sacred love!

If there be any heaven in earth, 'tis love,

Especially in women of your years.

Blush, blush for shame, why should'st thou think of love?

A grave, and not a lover, fits thy age;

A grave! why? I may live a hundred years,

Fourscore is but a girl's age. Love is sweet :
My veins are wither'd, and my sinews dry;
Why do I think of love now I should die ?

   Cup. Come, nurse.

   Nurse. Well, if he come a wooing he shall speed ;
O, how unwise was I to say him nay !   '[*exeunt.*

ACT V. SCENE I.

*Enter Æneas, with a paper in his hand, drawing the platform of
the city : with him* Achates, Cloanthus, *and* Ilioneus.

   Æn. Triumph, my mates ! our travels are at end :
Here will Æneas build a statelier Troy,
Than that which grim Atrides overthrew.
Carthage shall vaunt her petty walls no more,
For I will grace them with a fairer frame,
And clothe her in a crystal livery,
Wherein the day may evermore delight;
From golden India, Ganges will I fetch,
Whose wealthy streams may wait upon her towers,
And triple-wise intrench her round about ;
The sun from Egypt shall rich odours bring,
Wherewith his burning beams, like lab'ring bees,
That load their thighs with Hybla's honey-spoils,
Shall here unburden their exhaled sweets,
And plant our pleasant suburbs with her fumes.

Acha. What length or breadth shall this brave town
        contain?

Æn. Not past four thousand paces at the most.

Ilio. But what shall it be call'd? Troy, as before?

Æn. That have I not determin'd with myself.

Clo Let it be term'd *Ænea*, by your name

Serg. Rather *Ascania*, by your little son.

Æn. Nay, I will have it call'd *Anchisæon*,
Of my old father's name.

Enter HERMES *with* ASCANIUS.

Her. Æneas, stay! Jove's herald bids thee stay.

Æn. Whom do I see, Jove's winged messenger?
Welcome to Carthage new-erected town.

Her. Why, cousin, stand you building cities here,
And beautifying the empire of this queen,
While Italy is clean out of thy mind?
Too, too forgetful of thine own affairs,
Why wilt thou so betray thy son's good hap?
The king of gods sent me from highest heav'n,
To sound this angry message in thine ears:
Vain man, what monarchy expect'st thou here?
Or with what thought sleep'st thou on Lybia's shore?
If that all glory hath forsaken thee,
And thou despise the praise of such attempts;
Yet think upon Ascanius' prophecy,
And young Iulus, more than thousand years,
Whom I have brought from Ida, where he slept,
And bore young Cupid unto Cypress isle.

Æn. This was my mother that beguil'd the queen,

And made me take my brother for my son ;
No marvel, Dido, though thou be in love,
That daily dandlest Cupid in thy arms :
Welcome, sweet child! where hast thou been this long ?

Asc. Eating sweet comfits with Queen Dido's maid,
Who ever since hath lull'd me in her arms.

Æn. Sergestus, bear him hence unto our ships,
Lest Dido, spying, keep him for a pledge.

Her. Spend'st thou thy time about this little boy,
And giv'st not ear unto the charge I bring ?
I tell thee, thou must straight to Italy,
Or else abide the wrath of frowning Jove.

Æn. How should I put into the raging deep,
Who have no sails nor tackling for my ships?
What, would the gods have me, Deucalion-like,
Float up and down where'er the billows drive?
Though she repair'd my fleet and gave me ships,
Yet hath she ta'en away my oars and masts,
And left me neither sail nor stern aboard.

Enter to them IARBAS.

Iar. How now, Æneas, sad ! What mean these dumps?

Æn. Iarbas, I am clean beside myself ;
Jove hath heap'd on me such a desp'rate charge,
Which neither art nor reason may achieve,
Nor I devise by what means to contrive.

Iar. As how, I pray ? May I entreat you, tell?

Æn. With speed he bids me sail to Italy ;
Whereas I want both rigging for my fleet,
And also furniture for these my men.

  Iar. If that be all, then cheer thy drooping looks,
For I will furnish thee with such supplies.
Let some of those thy followers go with me,
And they shall have what thing soe'er thou need'st

  Æn. Thanks, good Iarbas, for thy friendly aid
Achates and the rest shall wait on thee,
Whil'st I rest thankful for this courtesy.

                    [*exit Iarbas and Æneas's train*

Now will I haste unto Lavinian shore,
And raise a new foundation to old Troy.
Witness the gods, and witness heaven and earth,
How loth I am to leave these Lybian bounds,
But that eternal Jupiter commands.

               Enter DIDO.

  Dido. I fear I saw Æneas' little son,
Led by Achates to the Trojan fleet
If it be so, his father means to fly;
But here he is; now, Dido, try thy wit.

              Enter ÆNEAS.

Æneas, wherefore go thy men aboard?
Why are thy ships new rigg'd? Or to what end
Launch'd from the haven, lie they in the road?
Pardon me, though I ask; love makes me ask.

  Æn. O, pardon me, if I resolve thee why;
Æneas will not feign with his dear love;
I must from hence: this day, swift Mercury,
When I was laying a platform for these walls,
Sent from his father Jove, appear'd to me,

And in his name rebuk'd me bitterly,
For ling'ring here, neglecting Italy.

Dido. But yet Æneas will not leave his love.

Æn. I am commanded, by immortal Jove,
To leave this town, and pass to Italy,
And therefore must of force.

Dido. These words proceed not from Æneas' heart.

Æn. Not from my heart, for I can hardly go;
And yet I may not stay. Dido, farewell!

Dido. Farewell! is this the mends for Dido's love?
Do Trojans use to quit their lovers thus?
Fare well may Dido, so Æneas stay;
I die, if my Æneas say farewell!

Æn. Then let me go, and never say farewell.
Let me go; farewell! I must from hence.

Dido. These words are poison to poor Dido's soul:
O, speak like my Æneas, like my love.
Why look'st thou toward the sea? The time hath been
When Dido's beauty chang'd thine eye to her.
Am I less fair, than when thou saw'st me first?
O, then, Æneas, 'tis for grief of thee.
Say thou wilt stay in Carthage with thy queen,
And Dido's beauty will return again.
Æneas, say, how can'st thou take thy leave?
Wilt thou kiss Dido? O, thy lips have sworn
To stay with Dido: can'st thou take her hand?
Thy hand and mine have plighted mutual faith,
Therefore, unkind Æneas, must thou say,
Then let me go, and never say farewell.

Æn. O, Queen of Carthage, wert thou ugly black,

Æneas could not choose but hold thee dear :
Yet must he not gainsay the gods' behest.

   Dido. The gods ! what gods be those that seek my death ?
Wherein have I offended Jupiter,
That he should take Æneas from mine arms ?
O, no, the gods weigh not what lovers do ;
It is Æneas calls Æneas hence,
And woeful Dido, by these blubber'd cheeks,
By this right hand, and by our spousal rights,
Desires Æneas to remain with her ;
Si bene quid de te merui, fuit aut tibi quidquam
Dulce meum, miserere domûs labentis : et istam
Oro, si quis adhuc precibus locus, exue mentem.

   Æn. *Desine meque tuis incendere teque querelis:*
*Italiam non sponte sequor.**

   Dido. Hast thou forgot how many neighbour kings
Were up in arms, for making thee my love ?
How Carthage did rebel, Iarbas storm,
And all the world call'd me a second Helen,
For being entangl'd by a stranger's looks ;
So thou would'st prove as true as Paris did,
Would, as fair Troy was, Carthage might be sack'd,
And I be call'd a second Helena.
Had I a son by thee, the grief were less,
That I might see Æneas in his face :
Now if thou goest, what can'st thou leave behind,
But rather will augment than ease my woe ?

   Æn. In vain, my love, thou spend'st thy fainting breath,

---

     * Virgil, lib iv.

If words might move me, I were overcome.

    Dido. And wilt thou not be mov'd with Dido's words?
Thy mother was no goddess, perjur'd man !
Nor Dardanus the author of thy stock ;
But thou art sprung from Scythian Caucasus,
And tigers of Hyrcania gave thee suck.
Ah, foolish Dido ! to forbear this long !
Wast thou not wreck'd upon this Lybian shore,
And cam'st to Dido like a fisher swain ?
Repair'd not I thy ships, made thee a king,
And all thy needy followers noblemen ?
O serpent ! that came creeping from the shore,
And I for pity harbour'd in my bosom ;
Wilt thou now slay me with thy venom'd sting,
And hiss at Dido for preserving thee ?
Go, go, and spare not ; seek out Italy :
I hope, that that which love forbids me do,
The rocks and sea-gulls will perform at large,
And thou shalt perish in the billows' ways,
To whom poor Dido doth bequeath revenge :
Aye, traitor ! and the waves shall cast thee up,
Where thou and false Achates first set foot ;
Which, if it chance, I'll give ye burial,
And weep upon your lifeless carcases,
Though thou nor he will pity me a whit.
Why star'st thou in my face ?   If thou wilt stay,
Leap in mine arms ; mine arms are open wide ;
If not, turn from me, and I'll turn from thee :
For though thou hast the power to say, farewell !
I have not power to stay thee.—[*exit Æneas.*] Is he gone ?

Aye, but he'll come again; he cannot go;
He loves me too, too well to serve me so:
Yet he that in my sight would not relent,
Will, being absent, be obdurate still:
By this is he got to the water-side;
And see, the sailors take him by the hand;
But he shrinks back; and now, rememb'ring me,
Returns amain: welcome, welcome, my love!
But where's Æneas?   Ah! he's gone, he's gone!

Enter ANNA.

 Anna. What means my sister, thus to rave and cry?
 Dido. O Anna! my Æneas is aboard,
And, leaving me, will sail to Italy.
Once did'st thou go, and he came back again;
Now bring him back, and thou shalt be a queen,
And I will live a private life with him.
 Anna. Wicked Æneas!
 Dido. Call him not wicked, sister; speak him fair,
And look upon him with a mermaid's eye:
Tell him, I never vow'd at Aulis' gulf
The desolation of his native Troy,
Nor sent a thousand ships unto the walls,
Nor ever violated faith to him;
Request him gently, Anna, to return:
I crave but this,—he stay a tide or two,
That I may learn to bear it patiently:
If he depart thus suddenly, I die.
Run, Anna, run! stay not to answer me.
 Anna. I go, fair sister! heaven grant good success! [*exit.*

Enter the NURSE.

Nurse. O Dido! your little son Ascanius
Is gone! He lay with me last night,
And in the morning he was stol'n from me.
I think, some fairies have beguil'd me.

Dido. O cursed hag and false dissembling 'wretch!
That slay'st me with thy harsh and hellish tale,
Thou, for some petty gift, hast let him go,
And I am thus deluded of my boy:
Away with her to prison presently!
Trait'ress too keen! and cursed sorceress!

Nurse. I know not what you mean by treason, I,
I am as true as any one of yours.   [*exit.*

Dido. Away with her! Suffer her not to speak!
My sister comes; I like not her sad looks

Re-enter ANNA.

Anna. Before I came, Æneas was aboard,
And, spying me, hoist up the sails amain;
But I cry'd out, 'Æneas! false Æneas! stay!'
Then 'gan he wag his hand, which, yet held up,
Made me suppose, he would have heard me speak;
Then 'gan they drive into the ocean;
Which, when I view'd, I cry'd, 'Æneas, stay!
Dido, fair Dido wills Æneas' stay!'
Yet he, whose heart's of adamant or flint,
My tears nor plaints could mollify a whit.
Then carelessly I rent my hair for grief;
Which seen to all, though he beheld me not,

They 'gan to move him to redress my ruth,
And stay awhile to hear what I could say;
But he, clapp'd under hatches, sail'd away.

   Dido. O Anna! Anna! I will follow him.

   Anna. How can ye go, when he hath all your fleet?

   Dido. I'll frame me wings of wax, like Icarus,
And, o'er his ship, will soar unto the sun,
That they may melt, and I fall in his arms;
Or else, I'll make a prayer unto the waves,
That I may swim to him, like Triton's niece:
O Anna! fetch Orion's harp,
That I may 'tice a dolphin to the shore,
And ride upon his back unto my love!
Look, sister, look! lovely Æneas' ships;
See! see! the billows heave him up to heaven,
And now down fall the keels into the deep:
O sister, sister! take away the rocks;
They'll break his ships.   O Proteus! Neptune! Jove!
Save, save Æneas; Dido's liefest love!
Now is he come on shore safe, without hurt;
But, see! Achates wills him put to sea,
And all the sailors merry make for joy;
But he, rememb'ring me, shrinks back again:
See where he comes; welcome! welcome, my love!

   Anna Ah, sister, leave these idle fantasies:
Sweet sister! cease; remember who you are.

   Dido. Dido I am, unless I be deceiv'd;
And must I rave thus for a runagate?
Must I make ships for him to sail away?
Nothing can bear me to him but a ship,

And he hath all my fleet.   What shall I do,
But die in fury of this oversight?
Aye, I must be the murd'rer of myself;
No, but I am not; yet l will be straight.
Anna, be glad; now have I found a mean
To rid me from these thoughts of lunacy:
Not far from hence there is a woman famous'd for arts,
Daughter unto the nymphs Hesperides,
Who will'd me sacrifice his 'ticing reliques:
Go, Anna, bid my servants bring me fire.   [*exit Anna.*

Enter IARBAS.

   Iar. How long will Dido mourn a stranger's flight,
That hath dishonour'd her and Carthage both?
How long shall I with grief consume my days,
And reap no guerdon for my truest love?
   Dido. Iarbas, talk not of Æneas; let him go;
Lay to thy hands, and help me make a fire,
That shall consume all that this stranger left;
For I intend a private sacrifice,
To cure my mind, that melts for unkind love.
   Iar. But, afterwards, will Dido grant me love?
   Dido. Aye, aye, Iarbas, after this is done,
None in the world shall have my love but thou;
So, leave me now; let none approach this place.
                                           [*exit Iarbas.*
Now, Dido, with these reliques burn thyself,
And make Æneas famous through the world
For perjury and slaughter of a queen.
Here lies the sword that in the darksome cave

He drew, and swore by, to be true to me :
Thou shalt burn first ; thy crime is worse than his.
Here lies the garment which cloth'd him in
When first he came on shore ; perish thou too !
These letters, lines, and perjur'd papers, all
Shall burn to cinders in this precious flame.
And now, ye gods, that guide the starry frame,
And order all things at your high dispose,
Grant, though the traitors land in Italy,
They may be still tormented with unrest ;
And, from mine ashes, let a conqueror rise,
That may revenge this treason to a queen,
By ploughing up his countries with the sword
Betwixt this land and that be never league,
*Littora littoribus contraria, fluctibus undas
Imprecor · arma armis   pugnent ipsique nepotes*.*
Live, false Æneas ! truest Dido dies !
Sic, sic juvat ire sub umbras.

Enter ANNA.

 Anna. O help, Iarbas ! Dido, in these flames,
Hath burnt herself ! ah, me ! unhappy me !

Enter IARBAS, *running*

 Iar. Cursed Iarbas ! die to expiate
The grief that tires upon thine inward soul :
Dido, I come to thee.   Ah, me, Æneas !   [*kills himself.*
 Anna. What can my tears or cries prevail me now ?
Dido is dead, Iarbas slain ; Iarbas, my dear love !

* Virgil.

O sweet Iarbas! Anna's sole delight;
What fatal destiny envies me thus,
To see my sweet Iarbas slay himself?
But Anna now shall honour thee in death,
And mix her blood with thine; this shall I do,
That gods and men may pity this my death,
And rue our ends, senseless of life or breath:
Now, sweet Iarbas! stay! I come to thee.   [*kills herself.*

THE END.

LONDON:
Printed by D. S. Maurice, Fenchurch Street.

CPSIA information can be obtained
at www.ICGtesting.com
Printed in the USA
BVOW11s0654270816
459972BV00006B/22/P